The War on the Other Side of the Black Abyss

By:
Juan Vasquez Rubio

Cadmus Publishing
www.cadmuspublishing.com

Copyright © 2022 Juan Vasquez Rubio

Published by Cadmus Publishing
www.cadmuspublishing.com
Port Angeles, WA

ISBN: 978-1-63751-173-2

DEDICATION

This book is dedicated to my children, whom I love and miss dearly. It is my hope that they read this book (especially my daughter, Mayra), and know that their father has never forgotten about them, throughout the 28 years I have been away from them. May God bless them all!!

INTRODUCTION

Heaven's Universe vs. The Kingson Universe...the oldest war...good vs. evil...God vs. the Devil. Two Universes, separated by the Black Abyss, are both thrust into the ultimate conflict. The Devil finds allies and shows them how to breach the Abyss that has kept evil at bay since the beginning of time. Humanity itself is the last hope of Heaven's Universe, not only in defending its existence, but also putting an end to the Devil's aspirations towards influencing the destiny of mankind. God and His angels need humanity's help to fight the physical and corporal threat of the Kingson legions. Retired General Aaron and his right hand [woman], Commander Malinch, must lead humanity's armies into the final conflict. Only with God and His angels do they even have a prayer to be victorious.

Table of Contents

PROLOGUE

At a time somewhere very near 2,350 years after Christ walked the earth, it was known that there was another universe that was different from ours. Although this universe was said to be far away, it was separated from ours only by an uncrossable abyss, where ideas such as time and distance mean very little. There was a Goddess who commanded this universe from her planet, Kingson.

All the inhabitants of the planet were known as Kingsons. They were tall and slender beings, with long slender arms of reddish color, much like the planet itself. They had faces and eyes that resembled that of a cow, and their ears were like that of a horse. They wore clothing as well, which was much like leather, and seemed as elegant in design as something we would see in our modern time(s), 2022.

The Kingsons were also similar to us in that they had humanlike emotions. They too suffered emotions. But unlike the Kingsons, we have a loving God that cares for us. The Kingsons had only a Goddess that punished and obligated them to do things that they wished not to do.

In the year of 2,350 A.D., following Jesus' presence on earth, Satan was still public enemy number one, against both God and humanity. He was also known as the antique serpent. One of his greatest threats was that he had somehow figured out a way to cross the Abyss that divided Heaven's universe from the Kingson universe, and in doing so, he made a pact with the Kingson Goddess. His plan was to attack the Heaven's universe and modify the Kingson race into one similar to human beings. In accomplishing this goal, there was only the question of when. Fortunately, our God sees all. God noticed that both Satan and the Goddess were conspiring a plan. He soon decided to put His awareness into action. This is when He advised His angels to contact the humans, in order to fight what would soon be a war on the other side of the Abyss. The humans obeyed God and traveled to the other universe, as God told them to. It was a terrible and unfortunate event. But everyone had faith that, in the end, through God, they would be victorious. It is my hope that the hearts of all who read this book will be filled with many moments of peaceful reassurances, happiness, and joy.

✦ 3 ✦

+ 4 +

CHAPTER 1

THE REUNION IN THE HEAVENS

2,350 years after Jesus Christ walked the earth, God, Jehovah, the Almighty Creator, and our Heavenly Father, called for a gathering of those angels that were closest to Him. He needed to explain to them what had been happening between the far limits of His universe and the Kingson universe, beyond the Black Abyss. He summonsed all of His highest ranking angels to tell them of the invasion that was soon to happen, as this was a violation of the highest degree.

In attendance were not only the many commanders of the millions and millions of angels that served our God, Jehovah, but the Angels Michael and Gabriel, and even the Son of God, himself, Jesus Christ. They were all gathered together in the Palace of

Heaven of the Grand God. Once upon His throne, He began to speak.

"Greetings to all," God said. "I bid you my most eternal love, which I have given even before any of you were created. The problem we have at present is that the Kingsons are intending to cross the Black Abyss and invade our universe, both Heaven and Earth. We cannot afford to let them cross the Abyss, as such an act will only turn into a war within our own universe. This is why it is necessary to come up with a plan to keep them from crossing over.

"How do they intend to cross the Black Abyss, when everyone knows it is impossible?" Gabriel asked, puzzled.

"Someone is showing them," Jesus answered. "Then we must have a traitor in the Heavens...!?" Michael declared.

"No," Jesus said, assuredly. "But it is the same Lucifer whom we all know that has learned to cross the Abyss, and now he is showing the Kingsons how to cross through."

Then our God spoke, "This is the same Lucifer who deceived up to a third of my angels, and, not satisfied with that, went down to Earth to deceive mankind, using his wits to take advantage of their ignorance."

He then continued, "Because of his lack of acknowledgement, even to my Son, who paid the ultimate price, humanity still suffers the consequences of the disobedience and lies of Lucifer. And now that Lucifer has entered into the Kingson universe, he is teaching the Kingsons how to defeat the angels of Heaven...."

But when Lucifer crossed through the Black Abyss, he should have been imprisoned and thrown into a dark pit.

The Goddess who commands all of the Kingson universe spoke with Lucifer and formed a pact and alliance. Lucifer, intending for this to happen, said, "If I am freed from this dark pit, not only will I teach you how to cross through the Black Abyss, but how to defeat the angels of Heaven." So, the Goddess accepted the agreement and liberated Lucifer. He then began teaching the Kingsons how to cross the Abyss and defeat the angels of Heaven.

God spoke again, saying, "Lucifer was once a powerful angel, himself, who was always close to Me. Even though he knew all the strategies of the angels of Heaven, he still knew that he could not defeat Me, The Grand God. And so, this is how he intends to try....

"The Kingsons are preparing for a grand battle on the other side of the Black Abyss. Ever since the beginning of eternity, the Kingson Goddess has always wanted to possess the Heaven's universe. But she could never cross the Black Abyss, ever since she was cast away and thrown into her own universe where she now resides...."

The Kingson Goddess had the features of a woman, but she was not entirely beautiful by any standard. She was between three to four meters tall, and her neck, alone was around one foot long. Her arms were similar to that of a human, and her hands had five fingers. However, her thumb and index fingers were unusually strong and could grip things with the force of a pair of pliers. Her legs were unusually thick as well, with giant

feet at the end of them, from which six fading red toes barely protruded.

Her skin looked similar to scales of a fish, yet it was as hard as a turtle's shell. She had eyes that were pitch dark, but with bright red illuminating from the center. Her eyebrows were as long and curved as the tail of a snake. Her mouth was like that of the beak of a snapping turtle, but with teeth inside. Upon it sat a flat, piggish nose. When she spoke, her voice was like that of a clucking of a chicken, and not much louder.

She had horse-like ears, and the hair on her head was as course and long as a mane, hanging down behind her head. And despite all of these animal-like features, her stature and posture still resembled that of a gigantic human woman.

The majority of her physical power came from her arms. The agility of her giraffe-like neck allowed her the ability to view approaching objects from any direction, 360 degrees, then strike at any angle or position. With every step she took, sparks spat up from beneath her feet. When she ran, there was fire. She also had the ability to combust other creatures into piles of dust and ash with only the power of her ill intentions. Because of this, and many more reasons, the Kingsons deeply feared their Goddess.

She had created beings with attributes completely different from those of the angels in Heaven. Their features were similar to those of the Goddess, but they were somewhat shorter than her. They lived in constant uncertainty, and they never understood the concept of the future. Because of these conditions, they were often restless and hostile. Otherwise, the Kingsons communicated mostly through body language and signals.

The Kingson Goddess had created a grand empire on her planet and in her universe. Her universe, like ours, is huge and massive, containing richness and valuable possessions. But what it does not possess is wisdom and intelligence, such as the universe created by our Almighty God.

Her universe and everything in it was void of love.

Millions of years ago, All Mighty God had defeated the Goddess Kingson universe. When she realized she was soon to be defeated, she surrendered. God accepted her surrender under the accord that never again was she to violate the limits of both universes, and to never wage war against our God. And she honored these terms—that is, until now. Lucifer had crossed over the Abyss, and deceived the Kingson Goddess for his own personal war.

CHAPTER 2

THE BLACK ABYSS AND THE BEGINNING OF THE CREATION

A place where angels cease to exist and turn into dust…

The Abyss is a very dark and dry place. And for certain reasons, both angels and Kingsons could not cross through it. For any who dared to try, they would be covered by a dark cloud that would turn them into dust—a state of total oblivion.

The Black Abyss was as huge and grand as any other universe. There was only one type of being that could cross through it without being harmed or affected by it. But the Devil, Lucifer, had discovered a way. It was a way that God knew even before the creation of His universe. And because God knew this, He created mankind out of flesh, water and bone.

By combining all these elements together, mankind would be immune to anything the darkness of the Black Abyss would descend upon them. He also found a way to conceal Himself inside of a human. He mimicked the human, and the result was immaculate.

This was also how Lucifer accomplished the task of crossing the Abyss.

When God created mankind, He made them superior to angels, and even the Goddess. But without the Spirit of God, the humans were like robots and zombies, and lacked any emotion or sentiment. They were not intelligent. Nor did they feel certain pain. In fact, they were often slow and dumb. But if they were to be injected with the Goddess's D.N.A., this turned them into rabid savages. For one hundred years, the Kingson Goddess and Lucifer created this false humanity, now known as the Kingsons.

The beginning of the human creation and the treason of Lucifer...

In the beginning, Lucifer was an angel of God. He was like the second in command in the heavens, but he soon after betrayed God while deceiving up to a third of God's angels. One day, God grew tired of his lies and duplicity. So, He ordered His angles to cast him out of the heavens. The order was mainly given to, and carried out by Gabriel and Michael.

Lucifer's exile eliminated most of the demonic and evil spirit, but not all of it. This was what created the war with Satan and his followers. The ones they could not save were already corrupted by Satan's ways. They too were cast out of the heavens. This is when Lucifer adopted the name Satan, and Devil. He came and deceived mankind, corrupting them along the way.

Those who were not angels, but mere mortals, were rescued to live in eternal ways, and in the Presence of God. But Lucifer, with his vengeful reign of a thousand years, was always coming up with methods towards deceiving and corrupting mankind, trying to lead humanity into its own self destruction. This he did because of his vengeance towards God. And this also led him to the grand idea of capitalizing on this vengeance by penetrating the Abyss and forming an alliance with the Kingson Goddess. It was known that the population of the Kingsons far outnumbered the angels in the Kingdom of Heaven.

Both old and new Kingson creatures were immortal. But, much like zombies, they were vulnerable to a strike to the head, should this disrupt any region of the brain. Black magic was how these creatures were created. So, as soon as the brain was ruptured, it would yield its life by turning into a 3-foot wide ball of smoke and disappearing, all within a few short seconds.

This was the only way to defeat the Kingson beings. This was the only way to eliminate the Kingson armies. War was the only reason for which these creatures were created, quite unlike mankind. They were programmed to jump high and far, almost as if they were flying. They could sprint as fast as 50 miles per hour. But every creature and being has its own weaknesses, especially not having what God bestows unto His creations.

CHAPTER 3

JOURNEY TO THE EARTH

God orders the journey to Earth...

God sent Michael and Gabriel to Earth, seeking help by speaking to the humans about the imminent threat of combat with the Kingsons in their own universe. But Michael was puzzled.

"How can this be that we are asking for help from humans?" Michael asked God. "Men are inferior to us, they have no power and are not eternal, like us!? They are mortal."

God answered, "Yes, it is true that men are not eternal and it is true that man is mortal. But he is only mortal on his own planet. If mankind is willing to accept my petition, they will discover that they are made of elements that the Black Abyss cannot destroy or surmount. I have made this so from the beginning of time."

Naturally, the angels were surprised to hear that humans could cross the Abyss unharmed.

"There is little gravity in the Kingson universe, and upon entering into it, man is stronger in certain ways. And what they lack in numbers, they make up for in intelligence and determination, far more than the Kingsons," God explained. "For these, and other reasons, we will send man over to the Kingson universe...."

Then Gabriel said, "But Lord, I still feel that man is not well enough equipped to travel so far to the other universe. Their transportation ships can barely travel from planet to planet in their local system near Earth...!"

"I know," God replied. "But we will equip them with other ships, and arm them well enough to combat the Kingsons in their universe. We will have to make them understand that this invasion that the Kingsons are planning is severely threatening to them as well. It is important that we wipe out that entire race, and liberate this universe from Lucifer's and the Goddess's designs. In doing so, this will be one less enemy against our universe...

"God then placed Jesus in charge of the entire mission against the Kingson universe and all that lives within it. But before setting out on the journey, Jesus asked," But, Father, God, with whom among the leaders of Earth shall I speak?"

God answered, "You shall speak to all of Earth as one. As you are doing this, I shall choose and reveal one man and one woman who will lead the human race on their voyage."

And so, God searched for the two humans that he felt would best perform the task. They were on a mission to Mars. God noticed them from the Heavens, as He saw that they were spreading the Word of God and were dedicated to leading others towards the road to salvation.

The man's name was Aaron Cruz, and the woman's name was Malinch Jones.

God said, "I will wait until they are done with their mission, because salvation is most important to the human race. Once they return to Earth, we will speak to them." Then, six months later, both Aaron and Malinch returned to Earth. Aaron lived in San Francisco, just north of the Golden Gate Bridge. He was a widower with a daughter of six years old.

Malinch resided in Michigan, very close to the Great Lakes. She was never married. Right from the moment He saw them, God knew that both Aaron and Malinch were the perfect ones for the mission. Out of the many millions of people, they were the most worthy, and they possessed all the attributes that He most wanted and needed for the success of this mission, in body, soul, and spirit.

❖   ❖   ❖

Aaron had become a widower after losing his wife in an accidental plane crash. Thereafter, it was just him and his daughter, Glory. He gave her that name because, for him, she was his glory. He would often say, "My wife is my heaven, and my daughter is my glory." He was an honest, humble, and amiable gentleman, always caring for his daughter and himself, with a very positive attitude. Being a man of God, he made himself very accessible to others, always offering them a genuine smile. At the age of 40, he is often found preaching in churches. On top of all of this, he was also very brave.

Aaron served in the Armed Forces for almost ten years, first in the infantry, and then as a pilot. Regardless of what mission he was on or what war machine he was operating, he was always victorious, due to his trust and faith in God. And God had confidence in him.

Both Aaron and Malinch worked for the same organization, called, The Holy Word. They were often sent to other planets, and their primary mission was to spread the holy word of Almighty God to other humans inhabiting these planets. They both became very dedicated to their work.

After losing his wife, Aaron had only a few regrets—one of which was not being with his wife before the accident. But besides this, and because he was very strong in body, spirit, and soul, he was very much at peace with all else in his life. This harmony made him the man that he is today.

Malinch Jones, though only 30 years of age, had very much the same personality as Aaron. She had served in her country's Armed Forces for eight years. She retired to do what she loved the most, which was working for God.

She lived a single life, and had no children. This made her more accessible to the needs of the organization as well, where she often traveled to the main office, located in San Francisco. This is where she met Aaron, and they both got to know each other very well. They not only became a very strong team, but great friends. Malinch enjoyed Aaron's company. In fact, she was innocently falling in love with him. She first noticed it when she was walking near the Great Lakes one morning and found herself in an inexplicably giddy mood, complimenting everyone and everything around her. So, from that point forward, every time they worked together, no matter where they were sent, she felt that she was the happiest person ever.

CHAPTER 4

THE ANGELS COME TO EARTH

God's message to Aaron and Malinch...

Jesus spoke to God, saying, "I have prepared all the transport ships and tools and weapons of war that will be used. But one question still remains, Lord. How shall I speak to the world as one, as you have instructed?"

God replied to him, saying, "There is a President in a particular country who is also a believer. I have spoken to him in his dreams. For now, be concerned only with sending my messages—one to Malinch Jones, in Michigan, and the other to Aaron Cruz, in San Francisco."

"Very well," Jesus replied. "I will send the angels

to deliver the message to both humans, and both Michael and Gabriel will speak to them. Once the two humans accept their mission, I will send them the war equipment."

So, Jesus gave the order to both angels. One summer morning, Malinch was wailing near one of the lakes, and two men in white garments appeared right before her. As they got closer to her, she could feel holiness radiating from them. Then they spoke.

"Glory to God, and may you have peace in your heart."

She responded, saying," Glory to God, and peace to you both."

The two men then introduced themselves to Malinch, as Marin and Corlin. "We come to deliver to you a message from Heaven."

For a moment, she thought that they were just men spreading the Word of God. Then they told her the message about the mission. After hearing this, she began trembling with uncertainty and fear. Then one of them gently touched her on her shoulder and said, "Do not fear this, for God, Himself, has promised to protect you...both Aaron and you." She became calm and peaceful again, especially knowing that she would be with Aaron.

After all was conveyed, the three of them stood together for a few moments in silence and solemn reflection. Malinch then took one final look at the beautiful scenery, before she would turn her attention towards the mission.

Later on, Aaron was met and greeted much the same way as Malinch. Upon hearing about everything—how the two of them had the task of leading the human race into battle against the Kingsons—he too was shocked and stunned. They made it clear that not another decision could be made until both of them were in full agreement.

Then the two angels reminded him, "In your mutual accord, both of you will be victorious. And it is also through this assurance that you will return. At this very moment, Malinch is on her way to meet with you over the matter. Once you two have talked, you will both be given final instructions."

"And she has already agreed to all of this?" Aaron asked. Both angels nodded.

Before Malinch had left for San Francisco, she began to feel nervous again. Overwhelmed by everything that was happening, she ran into her home, almost colliding with her mother, with whom she lived.

"My precious daughter, why are you in such a hurry?"

"I have to leave for San Francisco today," she answered, saying nothing more. She did not want to worry her mother over all that lay before her. But to herself, Malinch wondered if this would be the last time she would see her mother. But there was no refusing to do what needed to be done. For there was much more at stake than merely their two lives. Still, she reflected for a long moment how precious both life and family was. Both are priceless and irreplaceable.

That same night, Malinch arrived at Aaron's home in San Francisco. They wasted no time in discussing everything—how the angels, both dressed in white, appeared before them and instructed them on the mission.

"It appears that this is our mission in life," Aaron stated, courageously. "This is where we fight for everything we love and believe in. This is our God given purpose in life...."

Without saying a word, Malinch understood this to be true, and Aaron knew that she was in agreement. This is why God chose them, and this is why they accepted the mission—to fight to save mankind.

What also astonished Malinch were the millions and millions of light years this journey would entail travelling through. This made her wonder how everyone involved would be transported on ships that didn't have the technology, and were incapable of travelling such distances. Little did she realize that God had already accounted for this.

"Almighty God has spoken to our President, by some means. He, along with the two of us, are to speak to the entire world," Aaron stated. "We need to address the whole planet, and let everyone know about what is unfolding, and the imminent threat. But we don't have much time. It will be difficult to train all those who are willing and able to fight along side of us...."

Meanwhile, it was important for them to start heading towards Washington to meet with the President. Aaron's daughter was there, alongside a friend of theirs from Hollywood. Aaron hugged his daughter, and kissed her goodbye, before leaving her in the care of their friend. Although he didn't say anything, he too was wondering if this was the last time he would ever see his daughter again.

CHAPTER 5

GOD GIVES HIS MESSAGE TO THE U.S. PRESIDENT

God speaks to the President while he dreams...

So, while the President of the United States was sleeping, he would be visited by God in his dreams. God would say, "I am Jehovah, your God, whom you adore...the God you ask for help to govern your country as well as other parts of the world in times of hardship and desperation. Because of My help, you have always made good and sound decisions...."

God then went on to explain to the President everything that was happening and what was about to happen in due course. God instructed him to welcome and accept both the male and the female into his place, for they are both the chosen ones to lead the human race into the Kingson universe.

The President, in his dreams, would often wonder, "But how can we possibly fight and defeat such creatures who are so much bigger and stronger than we are? And do we even have enough time, resources, and technology to transport humans for a distance so very far away—farther than we have ever traveled before?"

God would then convey reassurances, such as, "We will give you all the technology and armament you need for this war." And though the President sometimes doubted the validity of the dreams, they became so recurring that he soon decided that they must be very real, very meaningful, and massive in scale.

The first transport shuttles were due to depart from Mexico within five months. But this first wave of ships were for reconnaissance, only. On the sixth month, the entire army that mankind had amassed would then depart on its journey to defeat the Kingsons and their Goddess, and if possible, capture Satan so that he may be brought back to judgment. He would then be cast into the Black Abyss forever.

After the President began to understand and honor the messages in the dreams for the petitions from God that they were, he then cried out to God, "You have created me in your image, and you have showed me how to love life itself, have appreciation for something as simple as a breath of fresh air, and the joy of laughter. These are all beautiful gifts you have given us. And I am grateful."

He then realized, much as Aaron and Malinch had realized, that he had a very huge and important role in all that was about to occur, and that this was his purpose in life. He then asked himself," How can I possibly refuse to help my country and the world?" He then accepted the part he needed to play in the mission, in order for others to succeed.

Not long after Aaron and Malinch went to Washington to meet the President, he was already waiting for them to arrive. So there were no misunderstandings or unnecessary challenges to overcome. After greeting one another, they immediately began discussing a strategy. First, the President needed to address the nation, then speak to the other nations' leaders. Afterwards, they would need to decide how and where to gather together all those who will have chosen to fight for humanity. Then they would need to be briefed and trained in piloting the transport shuttles, as well as any armament that was to be used in the war.

In six months, the entire human army was scheduled to depart, and to cross the Black Abyss, into the Kingson universe. By then, the recon groups would have vital intelligence.

Most nations decided to help. And although some other nations refused, in the end, there was a great turn out of over 200 million humans who agreed to join in the crusade. This constituted the majority of those who believed in the Almighty God. They gathered in what was the Gobi Desert.

Aaron was the Chief Commander, and Malinch was his second in command of the entire operation. One person who had perhaps the most experience of anyone, but who would also answer to both of them, was General Sanchez. Together, they trained every troop under the mandates of God's designs, as they all accepted God into their lives, and gave all glory to Him.

From the Heavens, the camp in the desert looked well orchestrated. Vehicles and planes constantly came and went, day and night, both from and to all places of the world, for various reasons.

Almost every day, new arrivals would be shown the objectives of their mission on huge TV monitors. And finally, images of the Kingson creatures they were to face, as well as their Goddess, were ingrained into their memory. They were assured that with the help of angels, they would be able to defeat them.

The Kingson universe had thousands of reddish planets, each one resembling Mars, to some great extent. Sometimes, a little stream of what could be identified as water could be seen. But there were no plants or trees. However, sometimes giant mushroom-like

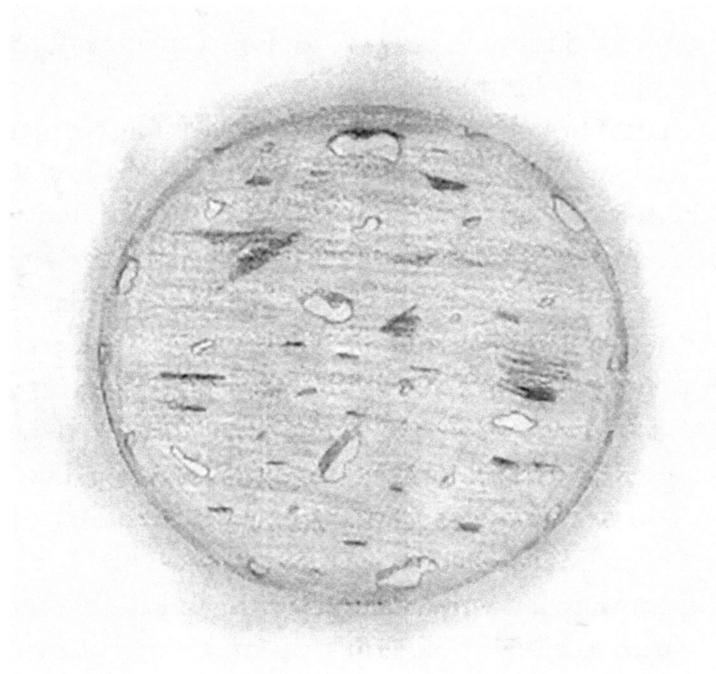

organisms would grow out and protrude from the reddish dirt. Some of these were as big, if not bigger than an average tree on Earth. And although there was no sun in which the planets orbited around, the landscape seemed as if anything living would burrow itself into the sand.

The Goddess's home castle, however, was as large as a mountain. This is where many Kingson creatures, along with the Devil, himself, dwelled.

Inside the castle near the Goddess's throne was a thick, white and reddish clay sand, as high as 50 meters. Since a sun was nowhere to be seen, the sand itself emitted a reddish glow. And, in no small way, this was the planet's light source.

No matter how big or small any of the Kingson planets were, it was well known that the Goddess reigned over them all. And the Kingsons feared her and obeyed everything she commanded. The Goddess reigned over her empire from one of three of the biggest planets. And it was this planet that would become the main target point for the humans. They would need to land there and attack it head on, and they knew how to defeat the Kingson beasts. Another thing that astonished both Aaron and Malinch was finding out that the Kingsons weren't even aware of what death was.

God was pleased with their progress, and all that they were learning. They took notes on everything, leaving no details to chance. They even took the environment of the Kingson planets into consideration. For example, the normal temperature on every planet was very hot— over 100 degrees. Also, the Kingson's armor looked like regular clothing, but, in fact, was very thick, like leather, and was a mixture of dark red and brownish color.

They also had to plan a way to capture Satan, and bring him back for judgment. The Goddess and her creations had to be eliminated entirely. This might be difficult, as the Kingson Goddess and Lucifer were rarely spotted.

On the planets, there were no winds or rain. Nor was there any wildlife. Every planet seemed to be lifeless, except for the occasional mushroom-like organism. Transportation vehicles were a daily occurrence, and sophisticated machinery was used to dig huge holes into the planet's surface to excavate fresh light source from the dirt.

The recon groups were identifying more and more movement, as if the Kingson armies were preparing for war. The war machines were much bigger and much faster than the transport vehicles. One of the primary weapons that the Kingsons had on their war vehicles were radiation guns—very similar to some of the weapons that the humans were using. So, the humans knew that they would have to coordinate an assault on the Kingson war machines all within the same time frame, to be most effective. This would be one of the key elements toward victory.

CHAPTER 6

THE WEAPONS THEY USE, AND THE WAYS TO DIE

The tools of war...

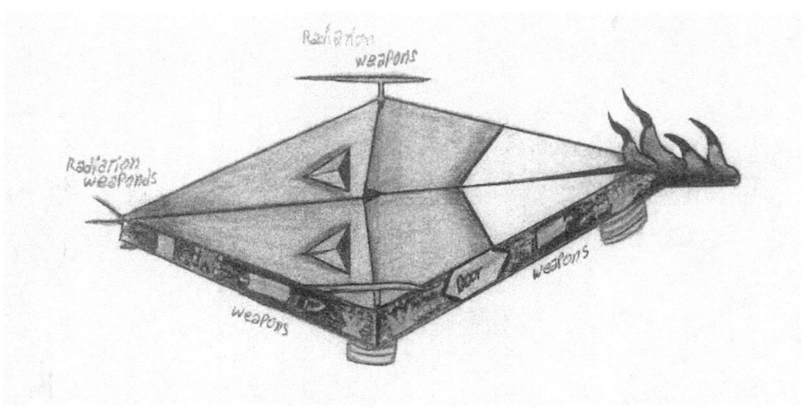

It so happened that the radiation guns that the Kingsons were armed with were very effective in killing angels. However, when it came to humans, it was only able to stun them. The reason for this was because when the Kingsons first built the weapon, they thought that they would only need it against the angels in Heaven. But the Almighty God knows and sees all.

At the time, the Kingsons were ignorant of the existence of humans, and so they did not anticipate having to do battle with them. And because humans are made of water, flesh and bone, this made them more difficult to kill. And because of this, God knew it was wise to attack them in their own universe through the efforts of humans, and not angels. However, since the radiation weapons could stun the humans, it was also devised by the Kingsons that they would simply eat the flesh other humans after they stunned them.

Since the Kinson Goddess was so feared, her system of punishment for disobedience and negligence was the only system of discipline there was in the Kingson universe. Such punishment often took the form of either beheading, or she would combust the condemned with fire, into a puff of smoke and ash.

Incidentally, back on Earth, in the northern part of Mexico, more sophisticated celestial weapons were also being manufactured in order to equalize the strength of their technology and maybe even give the humans more of an advantage.

By this time, the Kingson Hierarchy was aware that the humans would likely possess enough superior weaponry to defeat them. And this grim realization created nothing short of a desperate arms race between the two civilizations.

Meanwhile, training on Earth would continue. The volunteer fighters were shown every aspect and detail of the Kingson army and its creatures. They were also shown how the Kingsons reproduce and populate their armies. This means of breeding was similar to that of an animal. And when their offspring were born, they were born with innocent and uncorrupted minds. It was only as they matured that the Kingson Goddess would corrupt their minds.

She had a very deep hatred for God. And she was very satisfied with the war pact against the Heavens that she had made with Lucifer. And, of course, this pact was also pleasing to Satan, as this was the perfect opportunity to exact his vengeance upon God as well. But there would be nothing that could happen that God didn't already know about.

The now volunteer soldiers of the many nations and languages of Earth still had many unanswered questions that they wished to ask Aaron and Malinch. And the two were able to answer these questions through the aid of interpreters. From information that was coming in from God, through messengers, and also through recon groups, it was known that if they were captured by the Kingson creatures, they would suffer, very severely. This is why Aaron and Malinch made it clear that it was imperative that everywhere avoid capture, at every possible cost.

When in the battle field, they were to consider themselves already dead, sacrificed to the cause. This point was ingrained into everyone's mind. This way, there could be no idea of loss, and thus, they will have no fear. This ability to give their lives for such a noble cause was an attribute that was very specific to the human species, and given by God.

Some other questions that came up were, "What are our actual chances of winning this war?" and, "Should we make prisoners of any who give up?"

As far as their chances of winning, it was entrusted that, with God, all things are not only possible, but certain. And as for taking prisoners it was decided that for any who surrendered, they could be placed in an area of confinement with high, wire fencing. Malinch said that God will help us decide what shall be best for those we capture. Still, Aaron and Malinch had their doubts about some of these ideas.

Thousands of Kingsons were trained to use communication systems similar to ours. Also, the backup system was similar to something that elephants use in the natural wild. The Devil is not only smart, but wise in many ways. He not only trained the Kingsons, but gave them technology that was far more advanced than what they had before his arrival. For this, and many other reasons, the Kingson Goddess and her hierarchy were very pleased with their decision to ally themselves with Lucifer.

With his help, they were able to discover many valuable minerals that could be used against the humans. He also devised a way to alter the Kingson DNA to replicate that of an iguana. In doing this, if a limb is somehow cut off in the heat of battle, they can simply regenerate a new limb, much as an iguana regrows a new tail after it is severed. After 30 years (or seasons), the Kingsons were considered to be fully matured into adulthood. Once they achieved adulthood, they would stop growing altogether. Still, never were any of the creatures taller or bigger than the Kingson Goddess.

The hierarchy of the Kingson army wore headgear that resembled seashells. This was as strong as a soldier's helmet. They also had slightly different weapons than that of the Kingsons. The headwear of a regular Kingson soldier resembled the plumage of a cardinal, or even a quail. Each Kingson platoon had 1000 soldiers. And the hand weapons they carried looked to be little more than a pole or a rod, about the size of a long, high-power rifle. The source of power for the weapon was in the middle of the pole. It too looked like some sort of seashell, but out of both ends, rays of radiation would shoot out. It may not have looked very sophisticated, but it was still an effective and formidable weapon.

CHAPTER 7

THE ACCIDENT OF THE SHIPS AND THE RESCUE

The collision of the two transport shuttles...

During some of the training exercises, there was a collision between two of the shuttles. One was landing, coming in from Brazil, and the other was taking off from the tarmac, outbound for Germany. This accident occurred at about 1500 feet in the air. And since this particular air base was close to the sea, one of the crafts landed in the water, and the other on land.

The collision itself sounded like thunder, as the two crafts turned into two large fireballs and fell. Within moments, responders were racing to where one craft had settled onto dry land, and any residual fires were immediately extinguished. At first, the doors of the shuttle were sealed shut by the damage, but once they were pried open, smoke billowed out from the cabins and compartments.

At this point, everyone feared the worst case scenario. However, somehow, they found everyone inside was still alive. Of course, they were very shaken up and disoriented, and some were seriously injured. But, amazingly, everyone was still alive.

As the rescue teams arrived at the crash site in the water, the shuttle was seen still floating, due to the material that it was built with. It was equipped with crash safety equipment and floating apparatus. However, the front half of the craft was broken off completely, as a result of the initial collision with the other shuttle, and it had already submerged into the water.

The rescue teams were very quick and responsive. Divers were deployed to search for survivors. Once they reached the front half of the craft, they saw nothing and no one. However, upon further inspection, they realized that everyone in the front half of the craft had all gathered into the pilot's cockpit, as it was equipped with both air and water tight seals, in case of such an emergency.

Of course, some of the ones inside were badly injured, and they were the first to be rescued. Still, there were no casualties. After they brought each person to the surface, one by one, they soon after began to hoist the wreckage from the sea. Everyone could see that it was badly burned—almost 90% of it was consumed by the fire. Yet, no casualties. Many considered this to be an act of God.

As they took the injured to the base hospital, there were cheers, mostly for the Glory of God. Of course, they also realized that their specialized training and quick thinking had played a major part. Still, after seeing the results of this crash, everybody grew very impressed at how safe the aircraft technology was. Even those who hadn't served in the Armed Forces were stunned, for they had never experienced any of the brutal hardships and images of war, up close for themselves—the casualties and fatalities of it all. It opened their eyes even more to only some of the tragedies that were certain to come.

During the training exercises, a well-known officer, Captain Marcus, was having a romance with Caren Rubio. It all started when Captain Marcus had a conference with a platoon and some other troops. Caren was a pilot who had arrived to the meeting late, due to transportation troubles. Her scheduled conference had just ended, and another had just begun.

Consequently, she had walked into the training room in a hurried fashion and unintentionally walked in front of the Captain. Everyone laughed. As this happened, the two made eye contact with one another, and both smiled at one another. It would become a foretelling sign.

She looked beautiful, even in her pilot's jumpsuit. She made a point of apologizing to Captain Marcus, and everyone else, for being late. He replied, "That's okay—please take your seat." He then spoke to the entire conference room.

"We are here to select the first pilots to fly the shuttles. These new 7.0.640 shuttles are state-of-the-art," he continued instructing and lecturing everyone. The session went on for about an hour, or so. And as he spoke, he noticed how timid and embarrassed Caren still seemed over being late. After the session ended and everyone was leaving the room, the Captain said, "Ms. Rubio, may I please see you in my office?"

Now, Caren was 30 years old. She was very intelligent and amiable to everyone. And this is also what captured Captain Marcus's attention towards her. But he had actually first noticed her when the two shuttles had collided with one another, as he was the one that oversaw the rescue.

Captain Marcus had also been a widower for almost seven years now. His wife had died of a rare cerebral infection, however, and he never remarried. He was a well read and punctual man from Europe who spoke in a respectful and humble manner. Caren, on the other hand was Hispanic in origin and culture. Somehow, they both felt the same spark of attraction for each other, and often enjoyed sharing conversation as well as affectionate smiles and gestures with one another.

Caren knew about his late wife. She also commented how she had dedicated her life to her career, leaving no time for marriage or family. She had a brother who was a doctor. He lived with their mother, who was retired, in San Jose, California.

One day, the Captain told her, "You once told me that your dream was always to fly to planet Mars and beyond..."

She said, "Yes—ever since I was a child."

He said, "You know, that was my late wife's dream as well." He then went on, saying, "I saw you staring at the stars last night."

"Yes," Caren said. "Everything in space amazes me. It makes me want to figure out what else is out there. I've always wanted to know."

The Captain then told her, flat out, "I want you to know that I think you are a very smart and brave woman, on top of being an incredibly beautiful lady."

"Oh, thank you," Caren said, taken a bit off guard, but returning the look of affection.

As days passed, the Captain would often write poetry to her. And she was flattered. So, yes, it was safe to say that they were falling in love with one another. Malinch and Aaron had similar feelings for each other. They too were at each other's side as often as possible. But training over 200 million troops was a monumental task. Still, through it all, they had faith that love conquered all.

CHAPTER 8

THE END OF TRAINING

The human being belongs to God...

Shortly after the training period was completed, all the troops began feeling even more dedicated to both God and the mission that lay before them. They would all hold prayer gathering, regardless of their separate religions—Protestants, Catholics, Jehovah's Witnesses, etc.—because the cause they were now fighting for seemed so much bigger than any of their theological differences. The cause was now for Heaven, their own world (Earth), and the universe at large. If they weren't willing to fight for it, then all would be lost.

They would also give each other reassurances, such as, "Have faith, for God will give you strength."

Apart from these gatherings, there were also other things being spoken of, as well, such as how it would be traveling to another universe and setting foot onto one of its planets. Some were already prepared, both physically and mentally, while others were somewhat intimidated by the images they were shown of the Kingson beings.

Meanwhile, answering questions became very routine for Aaron and Malinch. Fortunately, there was always a steady stream of fresh Intel coming in almost every day, from the recon units. Every morning, Aaron would say, in prayer, "Thank you, God, for the system of order we have."

The base was miles and miles long and wide, in every direction, which was necessary to maintain training for over 200 million soldiers. There was even a base stationed in the sea. The training was hard and tiring, but in the end, it would pay off. It would have to, especially when facing a different species.

Vast armies of humans waited in the desert for their mission to begin. Meanwhile, all the leaders of the participating nations were gathering together to discuss the concept of world peace. This was also what God wanted, along with the understanding that every human being needed to learn to love one another.

After the gathering, the leaders returned to their nations, in agreement with the need for world peace. But they also understood and agreed that sending their troops to the Kingson universe was a necessary measure in order to attain that goal. There was no escaping the fact that they needed to defend, protect, and guard their livelihood, as well as God's peace. This they all believed, after listening to the personal testimonies of Malinch, Aaron, and the American President.

At first, many of the nations' people were criticizing those who had chosen to go. But after many began witnessing images of angels for themselves, along with some other evidence, many began to believe, realizing the seriousness of the matter at hand. This is when even some of the skeptical nations began to join in the effort.

Throughout their ongoing and tireless duties, Malinch and Aaron became good friends with Captain Marcus and Caren Rubio. All four would perform their daily duties individually, then gather together to socialize in their leisure time. They too wondered what it would be like to travel to another universe and set foot onto one of its planets. And in the back of their minds, they were all aware that the celestial shuttles would be arriving soon.

CHAPTER 9

GOD SENDS SHIPS TO EARTH

The arrival of the Celestial Shuttles...

There were some journalists who were suggesting that the shuttles would never arrive. In fact, there was much controversy over this matter, as there was some evidence that supported this opinion.

God spoke to His angels about this situation with the journalists. But through it all, He was still determined to send the shuttles as planned. Once training was completed, more than half of the Earth's armies were sent to the desert, near Sonora, Mexico, and Arizona.

It was roughly noon, on a Spring Day when a loud, roaring noise was heard throughout the desert. The Celestial Shuttles had arrived, and they could be seen for miles around. Of course, one single shuttle couldn't produce such an immense sound, but 400 shuttles together created an unmistakable presence in the sky.

People's hearts began to pound, and the nervousness could be sensed throughout the local populations. The troops, however, cheered their arrival. Aa the airways were cleared, wave after wave of shuttles came into view. The ground continued to shake until even the last ship appeared. The sight of the Armada was quite a spectacle. But each of the shuttles were massive in their own right. Never in history had such a huge and coordinated effort occurred. And there was hardly a single soul whose breath was not entirety taken away.

The succession of it alone, was beautifully orchestrated, and everyone was amazed.

The first shuttle appeared so enormous as it landed. As they watched, Malinch told Aaron that they should address everyone one last time, in case some were having any last minute doubts. Just then, from one of the shuttle's speakers, it then beckoned aloud for Malinch and Aaron to come aboard. Meanwhile, the other 399 shuttles hovered roughly 300 meters above the base.

Then the speakers boomed aloud, "I am the Angel Gabriel, and I am here to deliver these fine shuttles to humanity for your noble quest."

There erupted even more cheers and applause. Then Gabriel spoke again, "May all of this equipment be of great use to you in defeating the Kingsons in their ill attempts to defy God's Will."

Then both Malinch and Aaron added, "We will do all of God's bidding for the purpose of keeping peace and order in our universe, and precious life continuing in the Heavens and Earth, for eternity." Everyone cheered, for God had already blessed them on their journey.

CHAPTER 10

THE INSIDE OF THE CELESTIAL SHIPS

The ship's communications systems...

When finally both Malinch and Aaron re-emerged from the inside of the shuttle, all the high ranking officers and troops were eager to hear more of what they had to say, and to know what the inside of the shuttle was like. To their surprise, Aaron was nearly speechless. But he did give an encouraging two thumbs up, and for good reason.

The shuttles had the ability to travel twice the speed of light, which even at this time, was nearly incomprehensible. They were made from a material that humans have never known before. Looking at the shuttles was like looking into an amber crystal, though it was still not possible to see all of what was inside, from outside. However, looking outside from within the craft, one could see the outside, in most every direction.

In the pilot's cockpit, or bridge, the control panels were similar to that of a normal ship, but much more sophisticated and elegant. The transmissions and communications were operated by a touch screen, and the images on the control screens were 3-D line graphics. The travel and stay conditions for the rest of the ship's occupants were nothing short of luxurious. They were First Class, and more than befitting of any human standard. It was truly a delightful experience just to be inside the craft.

Other compartments and enclaves of the craft were furnishings for other functions, such as maintenance of the craft—heating, cooling, water and food supplies, and the like—and were stationed side by side. Each of these rooms was about ten feet, by ten feet, and was enough to accommodate a small crew of about two or three. Then there were the missile rooms and their storage galleys, which were restricted by an identifying security system. Next to them were the fuel and power source rooms, which were mostly intricate systems and cells for harnessing solar power, for which the crystal-like construction of the vessel was designed specifically for. The crystal hull of the ship would gather the energy, and the cells would store it.

To give one an idea of the scale of the craft, the operational capacity of each ship could accommodate up to 5,000 people. In fact, each craft was carrying an assortment other smaller fighter vehicles and aircraft. The accommodations were truly remarkable, and it seemed that every last detail was thought out, with nothing left wanting.

Humanity had never been thrust into such advances in sophistication of technology, for there has never been such need

CHAPTER 11

LEAVING EARTH

The departure of the Celestial Shuttles...

The same night the Armada of shuttles arrived, all the remaining supplies of food, water, personal arms, personal and medical equipment, and linens, had been loaded. About 30 minutes after everyone had boarded and been given their stations and assignments, drills were ran to acquaint everyone with their responsibilities. Then, after everyone was settled in, Aaron told Malinch, "It's time to depart."

Soon after all the final checks were conducted, Malinch and Aaron had given the order for everyone's departure. On cue, all the turbines on the shuttles ignited. Aaron and Malinch's shuttle was the first to take off.

Then, one by one, each shuttle followed until there were no more left on the base. Upon their final departure, a sense of pride was felt around the world...even more exciting than when the shuttles first arrived.

Once all the shuttles were airborne and grouped together, they took up a directional bearing, away from the sun. When in darkness the shuttles glow like a light. Another one of the special features of the shuttles is that they can sense approaching objects, even things as small as a particle of dust. In this way, it was as if the craft had a conscious mind of its own. In a way, they would need to in order to navigate the universe at twice the speed of light, passing and circumventing all the different sizes of planets, moons, stars, and suns, and making all the necessary calculations to avoid danger. Such calculations would be beyond the capabilities of humans, alone.

Nevertheless, it was estimated that the entire journey would take no more than 12 months. Because it was well accepted that some people would go through fits of anxiety and depression, psychologists would play an important role throughout the journey, keeping them sharp and focused.

In fact, the shuttles were like big ocean cruisers, or even miniature communities. Since it was a co-ed environment, there had to be a standard of ethics and protocol with one another, men and women alike. But for the most part, everything was stable and harmonious. All went well. Flawless, even...at least until Malinch made an announcement. "We are close to 24 hours from the Black Abyss. Keep calm, and in another 23 hours, I will make another announcement. God bless you all."

CHAPTER 12

THE ARRIVAL AT THE BLACK ABYSS

The dangers of crossing the Black Abyss...

The Abyss was a type of dark and void chasm between our universe and the Kingson universe. No objects were known to cross it, and this is another reason that God built the celestial ships in the manner that He had.

As soon as the armada entered into the Black Abyss, it got very dark, turbulent, and hectic. It was like being in a big, raging volcano at night, dodging large rocks and asteroids. Maneuvering around in this manner, the pilots had to make sure not to collide into other shuttles. To make things worse, visibility was very poor, due to other space debris and sometimes huge clouds of dust particles. The shuttles even had a type of "wash function" that cleared away some of the obstructions that made it difficult to see. Still, when it wasn't like a volcano, it was like a tornado.

Caren Rubio was commanding a ship among some of the shuttles leading the armada. Captain Marcus was also on the bridge with her at the time they noticed that one of the other shuttles was on a collision course with rock about the size of a bus. She responded instinctively by coordinating and positioning her craft into the trajectory of the rock, making it crash into the right side of their vessel. This kept the rock from hitting the other shuttle. Of course, their craft was damaged, but not as much as if it had hit the other ship. As a result of her efforts, there were no casualties. However, a few of the crew were injured. It became apparent that these shuttles can sustain a lot of damage, on top of being highly sophisticated.

As for the extent of damage to Caren's craft, all the turbines and motors still ran properly. And although there were some fragile and sensitive parts of the ship that were damaged, there were plenty of resources to repair and mend those areas and functions. Still, both Malinch and Aaron would constantly remind the other pilots to be mindful of approaching objects.

Caren was an excellent pilot, and she was able to negotiate the rest of the voyage without having to incur any more incidents of that nature.

However, the Black Abyss also had a strange effect upon time. For some unexplainable reason all the clocks and watches simply stopped, and some of the crew were experiencing a sense of suspended existence, where time ceased to exist.

Fortunately, the navigation equipment was still operating. In what seemed like only a few days later, the readings indicated that they were almost out of the Abyss. But on top of all that had occurred, with the rocks and turbulent conditions, the temperature outside of the shuttles was now fluctuating. It would get unusually hot—over 120°, then an instant later plummet to -10°.

Malinch contacted the other ships' pilots and announced, "We all need to perform a full equipment, electronic, weapons and systems check...then we need to check them again, to be sure things are operational...!!"

Through it all, it was a very intense ordeal, but everyone agreed with her. And they were glad that she had the wherewithal to take command of such a difficult and demanding situation.

CHAPTER 13

THE ARRIVAL OF THE CELESTIAL SHUTTLES INTO THE KINGSON UNIVERSE

Entering the Kingson universe...

The last stretch of the Black Abyss was finally in sight. Malinch got on the Intercom and announced, "Attention everyone in all units. We are about to enter into the Kingson universe. We are less than 8 hours away, and there is the possibility of an aerial assault from the Kingsons. We need for everyone to report to their battle stations."

Then, when they reached the distance of two hours from the Kingson universe, Malinch made another announcement, "All Celestial Fighters are to now lead the armada...!"

Soon after, they found themselves within the Kingson Empire and were immediately detected. The Kingson Goddess ordered that her soldiers man their war vehicles and take up their battle stations in attack formation. However, the Kingsons had always anticipated being attacked by angels. So, the arrival of humans was a confusing surprise. The Kingson hierarchy scrambled to form an emergency meeting to discuss the unexpected turn of events.

When the Goddess saw Lucifer, she immediately approached him and struck him, shouting, "Traitor!!"

"I'm not a traitor," Lucifer insisted. "This is the secret doings of our enemy, God!!"

"Of what 'secret' are you referring to?" the Goddess demanded.

Lucifer then told her of another universe where there was a bright sun with planets that revolved around it. And that the third planet from it, Earth, was inhabited by a species known as humans who served their enemy, God. And these invaders are actually servants of God, sent to her empire. The Kingson Goddess listened intently.

"Tell me more," she insisted. So, Lucifer continued.

"On this planet, Earth, humans willingly devote their lives towards serving God. And every day, more and more of them are being born again into God's Graces, and reaping the rewards of Heaven. And though His favor, they have also become mighty warriors, with superior training..."

This angered the Goddess, and she struck Lucifer again, telling him, "I should have destroyed you! Why didn't you tell me about this from the beginning?"

"These humans can be weak sometimes, and many are incompetent. I never believed that they would've been able to travel such great distances. God surely must've given them the help they needed. He must've furnished them with all you see before us now in your own empire, for the humans are incapable of such sophistication."

The Goddess then asked, "How is it possible that they have passed through the Black Abyss?? Remind me. I can't recall if you told me or not."

"It is because these humans are made of flesh, water, and bone. The God who made the Black Abyss made it so these humans are impervious to its effects. He planned this from the beginning, as He knows of all things, past, present, and future."

This infuriated the Kingson Goddess to the point of striking the other Kingsons around her, out of rage. The other Kingsons in the hierarchy then pleaded with her, out of fear.

"Our Goddess—we must turn our attention back to the invasion...!"

The hierarchy Kingsons were a little smarted than the regular Kingsons. She knew they were right and then restated her command to alert all of the Kingson planets to take up arms and man their war machines, both land and air.

Meanwhile, Satan noticed that some of the Kingsons were now somewhat displeased with their Goddess.

CHAPTER 14

THE PLANETS OF THE KINGSON UNIVERSE

The Kingsons head out to war...

The majority of the time, the Kingson hierarchy was not in accord with their Goddess's conduct towards them. But, ultimately, they had no choice but to be subjected to it. This also meant following orders to fly off from every planet and confront the invading armies.

The Goddess also asked Lucifer, "Are you able to do anything to stop, or at least slow the invaders down? Can you alter their minds, or influence their thinking in any way?"

Lucifer responded, "I can do no such thing any more. Only on their planet is that possible. For it is obvious that they have committed themselves fully to God for the sake of their mission. And it is obvious that God is guiding them from within. Our only hope is to capture them. But we will also need a way to usher them across the Abyss."

Lucifer and the Goddess realized that the most effective strategy would be to capture as many humans as possible. So, the Goddess gave the order for the Kingson armies to fly to the entrance of Black Abyss, to confront the humans there. This was going to be an epic war between the two universes.

It wasn't long before the humans were able to detect the approaching Kingson armies. Aaron and Malinch ordered a quick stand by, but with weapons hot, and Celestial Fighters in attack formation. There was a widespread nervousness that could be sensed by everyone.

Before long the approaching Kingson armies were in visual sight. Aaron and Malinch wanted to get closer still. In an instant, their signals went off, and they were being engaged.

"Weapons hot—free to fire!!" Aaron shouted.

But just as he said this, he noticed that all the equipment was overheating. Little did the humans realize that the Kingsons had already been trying to shut everything down by heating up the celestial armament and equipment with their radiation guns. And the assaults were coming from all directions. Even the celestial shuttles were able to sustain only so much heat and damage before shutting down and crashing.

Aaron gave the order to secure a safer distance, until further orders are given. Fortunately, there hadn't been any casualties incurred yet.

Incidentally, the celestial shuttles, too, were equipped with high power ammunition. These weapons could easily puncture holes in the Kingson's war vehicles. The humans then coordinated their own attack, and as they returned fire, many Kingson vehicles and other critical weapons were crippled, shut down, or destroyed.

"We cannot slow them down!! Our weapons are not effective…!" members of the Kingson hierarchy advised the Goddess. "And now it looks like they are heading to your home planet!! They must know where you are. What shall we do??"

These Kingsons were already growing weary. They didn't have the mental fortitude that the humans did. But they still had a lot of fight left in them.

This was the first war of its kind. It was a strange, and in some ways, confusing war. Due to the superior training, intelligence, and reconnaissance of the humans, many Kingsons were falling. Of course, in any war, both sides take heavy losses. And now, one shuttle had already been taken down, breaking into pieces and burning before crashing into a nearby planet. Only a few onboard survived, but even they were badly burnt.

Then, a short time later, down went another. But this one crash landed on another Kingson planet, named, Toston. And though many aboard survived the crash, they were shortly after captured by the Kingsons. The instant the shuttle hit the ground, Kingsons were at the site, gathering human prisoners as they fled the burning shuttle. Some humans tried to resist. Some even went down fighting. But eventually, the Kingsons prevailed.

Still, God was able to see all that was happening.

The Kingsons had no jails or prison camps in which prisoners were kept. Only huge holes in the ground. And this is where the captured humans were taken.

As this was happening, Captain Marcus and Caren were flying their craft very near the planet of Toston, where the others had crashed. And following them was their group, Squadron 250. This was targeted as one of the main planets that needed to be overtaken. And a full on battle quickly ensued between the two sides for possession of the planet.

The Kingsons had very makeshift battle forts that the humans were demolishing through a barrage of aerial assaults. Rockets were flying from and into all directions. Within the fray, Captain Marcus and Caren had been flying low to the ground, and managed to fly past the huge holes where the captured prisoners were being led.

They were about to land their shuttle on the planet when they were suddenly assaulted from a nearby Kingson artillery base. But as their own aerial fighters swooped down and hit the base with covering fire, they were able to land.

Within minutes, Captain Marcus was exiting the shuttle with a company of troops. As soon as their feet were on the ground, Captain Marcus told Caren to take off again, and hover somewhere high above, but close by, until he gave the order to come back down.

The Toston planet was inhabited by millions of Kingsons, and immediately, heavy fighting on the ground commenced. But the humans were so coordinated through their training that not only were they not losing, but were even taking on prisoners of their own.

Interestingly, neither side had ever seen their opponents up close. So, the close encounters were filled with curiosity for one another, aside from the brutality of the fights. The humans noticed that some of the Kingsons were even small and young looking, as though children. This they could tell from the color of their skin, as a young Kingson's skin changes color as it matures. They would study, and sometimes touch one another, just out of curiosity. It also seemed that some of the Kingsons were kinder than others, while others acted as beasts.

In one instance, after taking several Kingson soldiers prisoner, a human soldier noticed that some of the male Kingsons were assaulting a female Kingson. The human drew his sword and forced himself in between the female and the offending males, taking them all on, face to face. This seemed very dangerous, as he was vastly outnumbered. However, when other Kingsons saw this, some actually took his side, and stood with him against the others.

Of course, they couldn't understand each other's language, but they certainly understood the meaning behind the encounter. It seemed like they could identify the difference between good and bad. In fact, several other Kingsons took up positions close to the others, and gestured, by bowing their heads, that they did not want to fight, either. Other humans returned the gesture.

Both groups were very grateful and pleased with the exchange of sentiment. It seemed that everyone wanted some sense of mutual accord and peace. Meanwhile, the battle above raged on.

CHAPTER 15

TAKING CONTROL OF THE PLANET TOSTON

Humans take over, and Satan flees...

After the elimination and capture of millions of Kingson soldiers, the humans looked to take full possession of the planet Toston. Here, they would set up several bases as a military stronghold, and it was truly amazing how quickly they had done just that.

On the bases were prison camps, and it is here that several humans tried to communicate with some of the imprisoned Kingsons. Since verbal language would be too difficult, they first used signals and hand gestures. By this alone, they were able to learn that most of the Kingsons were not entirely cruel or mean, but more tame, as if a herbivorous animal. Their dispositions were a product of being oppressed by the dictates of the Goddess. She ran them into submission with the proverbial iron fist.

From one campaign to the next, the humans were able to overrun and overtake one planet after another. One high ranking officer that went by the name of Chapiro, took command of the entire planet, Toston, from and onto which shuttles would take off and land, routinely. Meanwhile, other aerial vehicles and machinery were maintained and inspected on a regular basis, as well, under the supervision of Captain Marcus and Caren.

Of course, the war still continued in other parts of the Kingson universe. But with every effort and battle won, the humans were advancing closer and closer to the main Kingson planet, where the Goddess had her lair. Aaron and Malinch were the ones on the battle front, leading the planetary invasions. They advanced like a big cat seeking its prey, and fended off incoming attacks like a mother stingray with her babies around her.

Their systematic strategy was putting more and more pressure on the Kingson Goddess. Even the Kingson hierarchy was up in arms about the human takeover of key planets. In losing the planet Toston, the Kingsons had realized that they had given up a major stronghold. Each planet lost after that was a regrettable reminder of this fact. Still, the Goddess tells them, "Keep fighting!! I refuse to lose my palace and my entire empire!" And the hierarchy would respond by frantically revising their strategies, over and over. But it was growing impossible to manage any aspect of the ongoing invasion.

Now, Lucifer has always been an evil being. At present, he still had an alliance with the Kingson Goddess. Deep down, he knew that the Kingsons would not be able to beat the human army and triumph over God. Still, he encouraged her to keep fighting. But she was no longer receptive to any of his advice. She grew so enraged with him over the continuous loss that she finally banished him from the palace, ordering, "Go do something to influence the humans' way of thinking!"

As Satan departed, he began thinking to himself, "If I can only find one weak minded human, I might be able to corrupt him."

He flew from shuttle to shuttle, scouring the minds of those within them. But he could find no one. Every human had the Lord's spirit within them.

In the sanctuary of His own Kingdom, God was seeing all that was happening. He then began communicating with Satan though spiritual telepathy.

"You will not be able to overcome my precious human followers!" God assumed him.

Satan replied, "There is no mistake that they have your spirit in them. But, I will overcome!"

"Leave now, away from my humans," God instructed. "Or I shall destroy you for all of eternity, and you will cease to exist."

Satan grew uncertain and scared, and soon he fled, all alone to a distant and remote planet. In the darkness of his own despair, he decided to wait out the war, until all the fighting had stopped. Seeing it any other way seemed to be a lost cause. He was abandoning the very war he only helped create. He was now a "wanted" criminal.

❖   ❖   ❖

Satan's next plan was to cross through the Black Abyss, where he could possibly continue his personal war against God and His human followers. But, being wanted, he knew he had to elude being captured.

Through all of the destruction occurring as a result of the battles, the celestial armada finally reached the airspace and skies of the Kingson's home planet. Even though it was heavily fortified the bombardment rendered immeasurable damage to huge dwellings and war structures across the surface. And though the Kingson army defended it with great resistance, heavy losses were incurred on both sides.

Many humans were captured while still in their vehicles, as the Kingsons were quick to simply throw any of their disabled vehicles into the detaining holes. The Goddess traveled west to one of these holes to exact a type of spiteful revenge upon any captured humans.

As a demonstration of her strange powers, she cut off a piece of her hair, and then mixed it with a yellow substance that she had pulled from a pouch she had fastened upon her side. She then mixed the two ingredients together and blew on it. A giant serpent suddenly appeared from within the smoke.

The creature resembled a prehistoric dinosaur, but was orange colored, with red speckles. It had the head of a huge bison, with a prominent snout, and a mouth big enough to eat an entire cow, whole. It was both scaly and slimy, and it hissed like a large snake. The tail alone was about 50 meters long, and frayed off into two menacing ends that seemed only meant for whipping its victims.

The Kingson Goddess then repeated the same conjuring gestures, and up arose another serpent, and another, then another. She called them Ajenjos. Only when there were many of them before her did she then gave them all a simple command.

"Defend me and my palace...and kill the invaders!!" to which the serpents slithered off to carry out her orders. Satisfied that they would do as they were told, she turned back towards her palace.

CHAPTER 16

JESUS CHRIST FACES THE GODDESS, THE SERPENT, AND THE DEVIL

The Serpents' havoc...

The serpents had encircled the Grand City Palace, to guard it from intrusion in any direction, for miles around. This was one of the Goddess's last lines of defense, before dealing with matters herself.

The humans were told through Intel sources that the serpents were there around the Palace, where they once were not visible or even existent. God also knew that these creatures could be of great detriment to the humans, and He spoke to Aaron, warning him of the dangers ahead.

"Make sure that no one gets too close to these serpents, for they are rabid and fierce. Fire your weapons from a safe distance if you have to. But don't get too close! Still, remember that every creature has a weakness…"

As Aaron was listening to God, the creatures were getting a fix on the humans' positions. Soon the serpents began devouring their prey, as humans unwittingly came within distance of them.

Aaron hastily sounded the alert to the other leaders, but for some, it was already too late. The serpents were wreaking havoc on the humans and destroying vehicles. Something had to be done. Until then, an order was given to fall back in order to reassess the situation.

God needed to come up with a plan as quickly as possible. He contacted Jesus, at the temple.

"You must travel to the Kingson universe! This is a war you too must fight in! Go defeat the Goddess and Satan, himself." Fortunately, Jesus wanted to be a part of this war ever since the beginning. And unlike the angels, he, too, was human. And most humans could not defeat Lucifer or the Goddess.

Lucifer, alone, was a very smart and crafty being. He cannot physically fight, so he uses his cunning mental influence to overtake his victims.

Jesus was also very familiar with his deceitful and conniving ways. He was also strong enough to battle the Kingson Goddess, alone. But the Kingson Goddess and her creatures would be more than a handful.

God constructed one of His fastest spacecrafts ever built. Meanwhile as the battle for the few remaining hold out planets continued, Lucifer waited patiently for his opportunity to cross back over the Abyss, to Earth. He had almost entered the Abyss, when his path crossed with Jesus's. They were so close that they nearly collided into one another.

"I am here to capture you, Lucifer!!" Jesus yelled.

Satan reeled back some great distance and shouted, "You and your so-called Almighty God are no match for me!!"

"Coward!! My vengeance will be swift," Jesus replied. "You will be judged for all your evil crimes against humanity."

Lucifer tried to flee, but Jesus's pursuit was swift. He lost not a step. Throughout the Abyss, he continued to chase him, until Satan collided with an asteroid, and became dazed. In that instant, Jesus took hold and seized him.

Satan struggled violently as Jesus held him in submission. He then tied and bound Satan with powerful chains and tossed him into the depths of the Black Abyss.

"For as long as my God reigns, you shall forever remain here! There will be no more corrupting humans!" Jesus proclaimed.

By this time, humans had taken over all of the Kingson universe except for the home planet, where vehicles and armament from both sides was blown into piles and scattered across the planet's surface. There were also wrecked celestial ships, as well as carnage strewn across the landscape.

Many were severely wounded as well. But it was incredible how few humans had been captured or lost their lives in relation to the amount of Kingson soldiers. For them, it ranged into the millions.

From a great distance, there was still a lot of artillery fire being focused upon the Kingson palace. But it was heavily defended. The palace was surrounded by a city, for an eight-mile radius in every direction. Overtaking the palace would be the final battle, to end the war.

CHAPTER 17

THE BATTLE FOR THE GRAND CITY

The dust storm and the serpent attacks...

A few miles outside the Grand City of the Goddess, an order by one of the celestial commanders was given to the human armies.

"Halt! Do not advance and further! The giant serpents are still at large."

Constructing a plan of attack would be necessary to lure the serpents out, so as to them fire heavy artillery at them, one by one. And though the serpents proved to be formidable targets, as agile as they were, the plan was effective.

One could see the gloomy entrails, as the human troops moved past what remained of the war-torn remains of the serpent corpses. The innards where the creatures had been struck were visible. The bones and flesh were different than anyone had ever seen, and the color of the blood was different. If they weren't created in such haste by the Goddess, they would likely have been even more difficult to kill.

Aaron and Malinch's shuttle, along with many other's, was still suspended high above, away from threat of ground assault. From that vantage point, they could see all that was happening, as the celestial vehicles unloaded their armament against the Kingson armies and the serpents.

Returning fire had knocked some of the human aircraft and vehicles out of commission as well, killing some, wounding others, and leaving these for whom it was impossible to rescue to the fate of being captured and taken as prisoners.

Serpents, however, took no prisoners. They swallowed their quarry whole. Because of this, any humans that were swallowed still had a chance of escape if artillery rounds happened to blow holes in the serpents' stomachs. Then any humans inside could be rescued as well, however much covered in the blood, slime, and vile that such gruesome occasions rendered. Otherwise, direct hits to the serpents' heads would drop them cold.

The Kingson vehicles were considered to be heavily armored. But whatever was left of the Kingson war machines were strategically positioned in lines, and moved only every so often to other locations. This was their newest strategy, as their stock had been significantly depleted. However, with the serpents' help, they had managed to dwindle the human army and space craft down, significantly, from what they started out with.

Aaron decided to come up with his own new strategy, by concentrating what fire power they had left upon a large hole from which many of the serpents seemed to be coming. Five celestial fighters maneuvered around, and bombarded the huge hole. As the serpents kept coming out, they were instantly destroyed.

This infuriated the Goddess. So, she conjured up a gigantic dust storm that swept across the desert and disrupted the stability of some of the attacking aircraft, forcing them to take emergency measures. But the storm affected the Kingsons as well.

Still, the battle continued, and soon the Kingson army was unable to hold back the advance of the humans.

Without the approval of the Goddess, the Kingson hierarchy decided to pull back into a retreat. They needed to fortify their final lines of defense. But most of the serpents had been wiped out, and there were far too few of the soldiers to have any real effect now. This angered the Goddess, and she doubled the intensity of the winds.

Dust and smoke covered the entire planet, and it was nearly impossible to see what was going on. The celestial ships hovering above had no choice but to rise higher, so as to remain out of harm's way. The troops on the surface took up shelter in their grounded ships. Even the Kingsons were helpless but to take up cover against the storm.

The winds were so strong that the debris was becoming deadly for humans. They also sought shelter within caravans of vehicles huddled together. But this soon became even more dangerous, as what few serpents remained were now slithering their way towards these shelters.

The recon teams and watch posts around the encampments found themselves fending off the advance of the gruesome beasts. Even those that tried to flee were caught up in the whipping tail on one side and the devouring jaws on another. When those inside saw what was happening, they teamed up and fired upon the serpents with what weapons they had. To their amazement, this seemed to work. Within minutes, they were able to neutralize and kill off any intruding serpents. Several humans were seriously hurt, but, fortunately, they would live through the ordeal, as the others tended to their wounds.

Still, everyone stood by, awaiting their advance. Their last obstacle was to now capture the city and its Goddess.

After assessing the futility of the situation, a group of Kingson hierarchy decided to send up a plume of white smoke, signaling their surrender. Many of the humans didn't know what it meant. But Malinch did.

"It's a signal of surrender!!" she exclaimed.

CHAPTER 18

THE SMOKE OF SURRENDER

The newborn Kingson babies, the thick water, and the fury of the Goddess...

Following the discharge of white smoke, the Kingson hierarchy was approached by the commanders of the human armies. It was agreed that they would be placed in prison detainment camps, once the storms died down. Capturing the Goddess wasn't going to be so easy. This is why God had sent Jesus, for he had the mental and spiritual fortitude to capture her.

The Kingsons, on the other hand, were surprisingly compliant. In their observations, the humans noticed that the Kingsons foraged for food in the ground, pulling up strains of fiber that looked like the roots of a plant. The giant mushrooms were also a common delicacy to the Kingsons.

Among the surrendered Kingsons were the pregnant females, as well as their young. And because they were deemed the least threatening, it was given them the privilege of venturing out to rummage for food and bring sustenance back to the prison camp. Still, they were heavily monitored. And there was still a language barrier between both sides. Only body language and hand gestures held any meaning.

Because of the need to maintain the population of the Kingson armies, there were always many pregnant female Kingsons going into labor. The female Kingsons always seemed very grateful of any help rendered by the female humans. It wasn't uncommon for the Kingson fathers to let the humans hold their infants.

The humans began to realize that, of themselves, the Kingsons were actually very caring and gentle creatures. It was also very disorienting for the Kingsons to be treated in such humane and civilized manner. What really stood out to the Kingsons was the generous supply of fresh water. They had never drunken such clean and pure water before.

Only one single Kingson soldier didn't like the water. After drinking it, he quickly spit it out before a human soldier, saying, "Chooki tany!" which meant, "I don't like it." Many other's eyes turned to them in what seemed like a tense moment. The human soldier then laughed in good humor, which made the Kingson soldier smile as well.

In good faith, the Kingson then gave the human soldier a taste of their water. It tasted like salty oatmeal. The human then spit it out and said, "Chooki tany!" This made everyone laugh.

Another humorous moment happened when a woman soldier kept having to go to the bathroom every few minutes as a result of drinking the Kingson's water.

Little by little, the brutal barriers that seemed to divide the two cultures were being melted away into a type of mutual appreciation and even compassion for one another.

Meanwhile, Aaron and Malinch were still in the shuttle, suspended high above the planet. They decided that this was the best time to surround the Grand City. They coordinated efforts with ground forces, and began a ground campaign that tightened their grip on the palace stronghold. Step by step, they closed in, closer and closer. But it also seemed that the Goddess would have nothing of it.

While on her throne, she created more challenges for the celestial forces to overcome. By simply closing her eyes and stomping her feet, she summoned a giant quake that shook the ground violently—equivalent of a 10.0 earthquake. Everything trembled.

Huge cracks appeared throughout the ground, so as to create a type of barrier around the city. Gaping chasms began swallowing up anyone and anything found themselves near one, Kingsons and humans, shuttles and vehicles alike. After it stopped, a makeshift bridge had to be built from whatever crafts still remained.

The Goddess, still determined to thwart every effort, then raised the thick Kingson water from what streams and pools existed. She then brought about great winds, again, that, together with the water, formed huge hurricanes that surrounded and pummeled all the city's occupants. The remaining armies had no choice but to take up shelter against the elements again.

CHAPTER 19

THE EFFECTS OF THE WATER

What water does to the planet, and what fire does to the humans...

Despite the chaos created by the hurricanes, the humans and Kingson prisoners were still able to weather the torment. It had never rained on the Kingson planet before, so what the water did to the surface of the planet was entirely unforeseeable. As the water hit the ground, it sizzled and steamed, as though dousing a flame, before sending up huge plumes of orange smoke into the atmosphere. The vapor was so thick that the humans couldn't breathe, and had to cover their eyes, mouths, and noses, while gasping for air.

A member of the Kingson hierarchy approached a human commander, saying. "Diera mach mua," meaning, "the Goddess will continue to do even worse." Unfortunately, the commander couldn't understand what he was saying, but he understood that the Kingson was trying to help.

The commander contacted Aaron and Malinch and relayed to them all that was happening. It was imperative that all humans take immediate and temporary shelter in the shuttles, while making sure that the Kingsons were cared for as well.

"Fire upon the palace while this is taking place, to prevent the Goddess from creating any more mayhem," he told Aaron and Malinch. But as soon as the shuttles started firing upon the palace, chunks of the planet began to hurl into the air towards the celestial crafts. However, the torrential rains were dissolving the boulders into mud before they could reach the aircraft, rendering them harmless.

Meanwhile, she sent out drones to scour the planet surface to obliterate anything that moved. The order was given by the ground forces that no one was to go outside, so no one could be seen by the drones.

The only movement her drones picked up was movement from the humans' drones.

CHAPTER 20

AARON SEEKS A MESSAGE FROM GOD

The Goddess's last line of defense...

In another effort to thwart the humans, the Goddess then set the ground on fire. It was no surprise that the flames seemed to have a life of their own. The humans quickly gathered together and coordinated an effort with air support to extinguish the flames. This took what seemed like days, but it was finally put out. The skies were clear again, at least for now.

Aaron and Malinch then sent a message to the commanders on the ground. "We're going to advance into the city. Advise all ground forces to advance as well."

The Goddess had a mere handful of devoted followers left in the city. As the humans entered, the ground war intensified again. In many places, it resorted to hand-to-hand combat. Radiation blasts were rendering many humans unconscious, and susceptible to capture. The humans feared capture more than dying, because it was rumored that they were being tortured and not cared for at all. Tension was reaching another critical point in the war.

The gear that the ground forces wore protected them from head to toe. But they were still as susceptible to injury from the Kingsons in hand-to-hand combat as the Kingsons were likely to fall at the hands of human ingenuity. Incidentally, one of the ground commanders, Captain Tilley, kept reminding the ground forces to fire headshots, only.

Throughout the city, Kingsons were being defeated. Kingson homes and city dwellings that were made of reddish clay, were being devastated and leveled into rubble. Relentlessly, the humans fought, and closer and closer, they came to the Grand Palace. Eventually, all the Kingsons in the city were defeated. All that was left was the Goddess, herself, and the few Kingson soldiers surrounding her inside.

There was a huge wall that made up the perimeter of the palace. It was full of hidden traps and hazards. Fearing any unforeseeable tricks that the Goddess might still have, Aaron gave an order to all the forces, "Do not attempt to enter the palace—only surround it!" The celestial shuttles hovered overhead, but no one was to fire a single shot until told to.

Aaron was very reluctant about putting any more human lives at stake, especially against the Goddess. He felt he had no choice but to seek advice from the Heavens, through a prayer to God, Almighty.

It said, "Dear Almighty God of the Heavens above, to Whom I give all glory. With great humility, I beseech your help, for we have done all you have instructed to defeat the Goddess. But the situation that we presently face is beyond our capability. How do you expect us to defeat the powerful Goddess? We need your help."

God responded. "Have faith, and do not worry. I will send one who shall arrive soon and capture the Goddess. Just wait and have trust and confidence in Me."

After Aaron conveyed this message to Malinch and some of the other commanders, they started to wonder who it was that God would send. Someone said, "Well, we shouldn't forget that Jesus was also a human born on Earth..."

CHAPTER 21

CHRIST IS CALLED TO THE KINGSON UNIVERSE TO TAKE THE GODDESS

Jesus Christ comes for the Kingson Goddess...

Jesus is a powerful man. He does not need wings to fly. He sees all that is both physical and spiritual, visible and invisible. Not only was he betrayed by Judas, but he was innocently sentenced to death by the corruption and envy of others. This is what led to his crucifixion. This was his grand sacrifice for the salvation of all men. He was then resurrected on the third day, and the first human to live in the Heavens with God. This was prophecy, fulfilled by the King of Kings. He's our savior. He's the son of God.

As for the Goddess, he will capture her and see her judgment through, much as he had thrown Satan, chained and bound, into the Abyss.

At the time of Jesus' arrival, the Goddess had three members of the Kingson hierarchy left with her, and a mere thousand more Kingson fighters left inside the palace. She also possessed the power to conjure up monstrous creatures and catastrophes, which, alone, was still enough to make it difficult to enter.

The human soldiers had been waiting for Jesus to arrive, so that they might lift the order to stand by, and assist in storming and raiding the palace. Still, the huge wall needed to be torn down for them to help.

An order was given to clear the west side of the palace so that Aaron and Malinch's shuttle might descend and land. Once they did, many humans rejoiced, as it had been a long and arduous war—what felt like years to many. Some human soldiers hadn't had contact with each other, except for the limited communications on the army's network. But this wasn't the same as talking to each other, face to face.

The human armies had been through a lot. From one catastrophe to the next, plagues, creatures, and tribulations, and close calls with the shuttles, somehow they still had a very joyous and positive attitude.

Aaron then announced, "All is well—we will wait for our lord, Jesus, to arrive. He will tell us what to do next, and hopefully all this will end soon."

Just hearing this alone was enough to put the troops at ease and bolster their faith. They all knew that God promised to aid them in their victory against the Kingsons. And He always comes through with His promises to be delivered.

Meanwhile, the Goddess was growing angrier and more frustrated. She knew that it was growing impossible for her to elude capture. The walls shook and trembled whenever she yelled at what few Kingson underlings still stood by her side. They would only continue to suffer for their ongoing allegiance to her, through her rampant fits of fury and anger.

One Kingson servant approached her and said, "Dico mondy ova," which meant, "One ran outside," referring to one of Kingsons who had just defected. This made her even more angry, as it was an important member of her hierarchy.

One of the privileges of being a member of the Hierarchy is having vital information about the Goddess, including knowledge of secret passages and tunnels. This member had managed to escape through the northern palace entrance. The reasons were that he simply wanted to be free of the Goddess's relentless cruelty. But his decision wasn't just for him, but for his mate, and their newborn infant. His views were no longer in accord with those of the Goddess. He was starting to feel something different—what the humans called love.

His escape, along with his mate and their infant was successful.

It so happened that this defected hierarchy member was a high-ranking leader, third in command, after the Goddess, herself. When Aaron saw the family of Kingsons fleeing, he ordered that nobody attack. In fact, the humans signaled to the Kingson, and he seemed to understand what they meant. Once in the presence of the human army, the Kingson introduced himself as Zinson, and offered his rank in good faith.

"Why did you abandon your Goddess?" Aaron asked, directly.

"I refused to be by the side of the Goddess any more. Her idea to invade your universe came from a powerful spirit that convinced her to do so," the Kingson replied. "This evil spirit got into the Goddess, deceived her and manipulated her. It convinced her to build a pact with it, to invade your universe. This was how this whole celestial war was conceived. I often feared that forces from another universe would one day come to wipe us out. And that time had come with your arrival. I was then made to learn of your language for her designs, but decided instead to use of for the liberation of my family. She's grown out of control. She must be stopped!"

Aaron and those who heard the Kingson's story stood there, rather taken aback by his account. Aaron then ordered that the Kingson and his family's nerds be taken care of. Malinch then approached the Kingson family and began playfully fondling the infant Kingson.

"How can we gain entry to the palace?" she asked Zinson. "And are there any other dangers inside we should be aware of?"

CHAPTER 22

SECRETS OF THE PALACE

Zinson Tells the Humans how to get in....

You will first need to find a weak spot in the wall," Zinson began. "There are several most identifiably at points where the wall is the highest. This is where it is weakest. I know this because I helped build the wall, long ago," Zinson recounted.

"As for other dangers, there is a lake around the palace wall that will turn to fire, once you try to cross it. The only thing that can extinguish the fire is the red dirt from the ground. Simply throw it on the fire and it will go out immediately.

However, once you cross the lake, you will also receive heavy resistance from within the palace. There are

Kingson spirits that will hurl objects at you. And there is only one thing that can stop these spirits..."

"What!?" Malinch asked, paying close attention.

"Your God," Zinson revealed. "Only the One True Spirit has dominion over all other spirits. If you pray to your Almighty God, these other spirits will vanish altogether, and be banished into the Black Abyss. And the only reason I know this is because I have heard our Goddess speak of your God, with grave concern."

After hearing Zinson's account, Malinch conveyed all the Intel, and preparations to bring the palace wall down were made. Weak spots were noted, based on Zinson's insights, and celestial ships were fixed on target locations. On the ground, Aaron ordered other celestial vehicles to amass as much red dirt as possible into their carriage bays, and pour it into the lake.

As all this was taking place, a deep and foreboding rumble came from all directions. At first, the human army thought it was the Goddess conjuring up another storm or quake. But when everyone looked up into the sky, they saw none other than Jesus, in his celestial ship, arriving to the Kingson planet to capture the Goddess, for himself. In an instant, everyone threw up their arms and cheered.

As Jesus descended, he announced calming assurances, "Worry not, for I have been sent by your Father, God, to help you..."

He then met with Aaron and Malinch to discuss the situation at hand. Jesus agreed with what they had planned. Jesus was also able to see into Zinson's heart, and he could tell that he was not lying.

"This Kingson speaks the truth! You must all listen to him, and use all he has told you to accomplish your mission!" Jesus commanded.

Zinson instantly took kindly to Jesus, and everyone else was amazed how nothing seemed impossible or troubling any more.

"I have come to capture the Kingson Goddess and detain her before she does any more harm to anyone. I shall go into the palace first, and the rest of you shall follow me, and assume control over the rest of the palace."

Jesus then said a prayer for everyone.

"Lord, thy God, our Heavenly Father, give us the strength to be victorious in this final conquest. And let us put beneath us those that oppose you, and oppress those that worship you, Amen."

"I must go now," Jesus said. He then disappeared into the palace.

The Goddess had known that Jesus was close by. She could feel his presence. But never did she think she would find him inside her palace, that is, until he appeared right before her. When she saw Jesus appear, she became furious, and roared at him.

The palace walls trembled, and the floor quaked. Objects all around them fell to the ground, crumbled, or burst into a puff of smoke. The Kingsons spirits who hovered around her coward like scared puppies.

I am here for you all," Jesus proclaimed. "You have violated universal laws, pacts, and agreements, but none more so than YOU!" Jesus declared, pointing at the Goddess.

"No one will ever detain me—not even you," the Goddess said defiantly. She then bellowed a strident screech that pierced the entire palace, as the Kingson spirits flung themselves towards Jesus.

Zinson was then brought up to be awarded a human Medal of Honor for the pivotal role he played in bringing about the end of such an evil empire, and in helping to create an entirely new world brimming with hope.

Before everyone, he graciously accepted the medal.

The Counsel Members then faced Zinson and spoke again, "Zinson, it has also been decided that you shall reign over the Kingson civilization, as the new Kingson God."

Hearing this, Zinson was speechless.

"Never forget that the entire Kingson universe is now under your care," the Counsel continued. "Be fair and just. Have love for the Kingsons and they will honor your will, and obey your commandments. What happened with the Goddess shall never happen again. For as long as you abide within the universal laws, the Counsel Members will hear your wishes when you call upon us. And for as long as you hear the prayers and pleas of you Kingson people, all Kingsons shall know that you are Lord."

The Seven Counsel members then approached Zinson and gently laid their hands on him. At that moment, his body became luminescent, and he became clad in an elegant robe. Everyone was in awe.

Zinson kneeled down and vowed in his heart to honor the Universal Agreements of the Counsel. And seeing this, all the Kingsons bowed down to honor Zinson as their new Lord.

The Counsel then gave one last condition to Zinson, "Once you create your kingdom, you must help the humans return to their universe. They belong to theirs, as you belong to yours. This is universal law."

With those final instructions, the Counsel Members disappeared. Then as Zinson stood up, a great and mighty rumble echoed throughout the land. At first, everyone looked to Zinson in trepidation, fearing the power that had now been bestowed unto him. But he merely chuckled, which put everyone's heart at ease.

"So, what do you think?" Zinson asked Malinch, wanting her opinion of his new station.

"I don't think anyone here will need any convincing that you are their God," she said with a wink. Zinson smiled.

Zinson then faced the masses of humans and said, "For everything you have done in obedience to your Heavenly God for the sake of the Kingsons, we too shall comply with your bidding in your quest to return to your Universe. You are blessed by the Almighty God of the Heavens, and we are at your service..."

In his reign, Zinson wanted very much to emulate the designs of the human's benevolent God of the Heavens. This seemed a simple choice to make. He even went deep into space and created an immense explosion that not only brought forth stars in the sky above, but the arrangement one planet—the one where the Goddess was captured—that he turned into a star, and placed it so close to the Kingson home planet as to create darkness and light, daytime and night.

New life began to spring up from the dry terrains of the once barren planets. Trickles of water began springing up in remote cracks and crevices, and in some places, lakes and rivers were slowly forming. And around them, many of what would be called plush oases on Earth, were now cropping up.

What was once desolate red dirt became moist, rich soil, full of nutrients. Vegetation started to flourish, and flowers started to bloom. The Kingson planets would soon be flush with life, and the Kingsons had never witnessed such beauty.

Everyone celebrated the new changes with a new-found appreciation for life.

CHAPTER 23

AARON'S ORDER TO HEAD HOME

God's work is done...

Life was now flourishing in the New Kingson universe, under Zinson's rule. In every body of water, there were species of swimming creatures that resembled fish. In the sky, there were species of flying creatures that resembled birds, and throughout the land roamed species of climbing, crawling, and walking creatures that resembled the array of life that gave Earth its unique beauty. But on the Kingson planets, the vegetation was so nutritious and plentiful that all the Kingsons were essentially vegetarians.

Zinson never betrayed the Goddess. She betrayed the Kingsons. This was one of the foremost reasons for Zinson to create a planet environment that was in every way different from what she had created. It just so happened that everyone else was overjoyed by the changes as well.

After resting a while he rebuilt the inside and outside of the palace to make it more of a pleasant experience that everyone was invited to enjoy instead of a place to exalt himself with, or hide from his kingdom. The wall was completely torn down, and a group of personal representatives was chosen to care for the populace. When he was done creating his kingdom, it was time to return to his throne and begin helping the humans return to their universe.

Aaron had already given the order to clean up and dispose of all the war equipment that had for so long littered the planet's landscape. Memorials were established for those fallen in battle, and the Kingsons swore to honor them until the end of time. Soon, the humans would be boarding their ships for the last time, and there was an excitement and eagerness to do so.

Both Aaron and Malinch went to the palace once more, to speak to Zinson. Aaron spoke to him in Kingson language.

"Diece fuchon case gora ata dieca," which meant, "We brought the war against your Goddess, but now we are brothers."

Then Malinch spoke, saying, "We regret bringing so much destruction to your universe. For that, we are sorry. But for what we have gained in the experience, we are wiser and happier. Thank you."

Zinson accepted both their apology, and their eternal bond. Then they told him that they will be sending the first of the shuttles in short time. It was time for them to go home. But they could not cross back without his permission. Zinson then spoke to Malinch, saying, "Natuna tutub cardare cony ta dieca," meaning, "The Goddess wanted to cross the Abyss for selfish reasons. I will use it only for good."

Zinson continued, saying, "Although I was subservient to her, I never agreed with the Goddess's breaking of universal laws. We Kingsons have nothing but appreciation for you and the other humans for changing our lives. Before, we had nothing, as it was all for the sake of the Goddess. But now we have everything, all for the sake of something grand. I will thank your Almighty God, myself, for what He has given you. For through you, He has given to us."

"It was a great pleasure meeting you and becoming your brother," Aaron said. "I hope we meet again in the future. Just remember that I am only a mortal in my world."

Zinson replied, "It was a pleasure to meet you as well, and to come to know of your Almighty God's most beloved creations. I think it is incredible how far you have traveled for the sake of your devotion. I have learned much."

"The humans are not as strong as Kingsons in physical strength," Aaron responded. "But having faith is sometimes more important than physical strength."

Malinch had reservations about leaving, as she was so enveloped in playing with Zinson's infant child, Zoty.

In a way, Zinson didn't want them to go, either. But he knew they must leave in order for their happiness to be complete as well.

Zinson then stood up and raised his hands above his head, proclaiming, "Aty teta!" meaning, "Let it be!"

With tears in her eyes, Malinch then said her good-byes to Zoty. Then Aaron took Malinch's hand, and they both left.

Outside the palace, all the humans had congregated, and were bidding farewell to the Kingsons. The shuttles were close by, awaiting their departure.

After all the celestial troops had boarded their shuttles for the last time, hardly a few minutes had passed before the engines started to wind up.

"We are ready to begin our departures back to Earth!" the intercom blared. And all on the celestial ships cheered the most celebratory cheers, but also with tears in everyone's eyes.

"Check all your controls! We will be lifting off momentarily...!" the speaker ordered. "Double check them if you have to....!"

Moments later, the order was given for the first wave of shuttles to take off. Then the next wave, and the next. The noise was thunderous and deafening. The ground shook, and the air filled with the sight of celestial shuttles scattered across the sky.

Across all the Kingson planets plumes of white smoke billowed into the air, as celebratory symbols of peace throughout. As Aaron and Malinch's shuttle began to take off, they circled around the city, discharging white smoke as well. Then, in a tumultuous roar, the shuttles ascended into the sky above. Below, every Kingson was in attendance, watching in gaping wonder and awe.

As the ships took off, Aaron's voice came over the intercom, "The rally point will be at the edge of the Abyss..."

But after conveying this to the other shuttles, Aaron and Malinch diverted their shuttle to one of the nearby water falls that Zinson had created for them, in their honor. They wanted to get one last look at the planet and all it represented to them.

CHAPTER 24

AARON DECLARES HIS LOVE FOR MALINCH

Aaron gives thanks to the troops...

As Aaron and Malinch's craft hovered above the falls, they took the final moment to take in the now breathtaking spectacle that they helped to make possible, Aaron decided that this was the perfect time to declare his love for Malinch.

"Malinch, throughout the time we have known each other and lived with one another, I have held back the full breadth of my feelings for you. There has been so many things to tend to that it never seemed the right time to tell you how I felt. But I am unable to withhold my feelings any longer...."

Aaron then took Malinch's hand, and looked her in

the eyes. "I am more in love with than I have ever been with anyone before. Will you do me the honor of being my wife?"

"Yes! Of course!" Malinch responded in giddy excitement. "Before you even loved me, I was already in love with you!"

"When we get back to Earth, we'll get married! I'm sure that my daughter will absolutely love you as a mother to her...!"

The two then kissed for a long time. After spending a few long moments with each other, staring into each other's eyes, they decided that they should get going, to catch up to the rest of the fleet.

That night, Aaron spoke to all the shuttle crews over the open intercom and videos monitors. Everyone stood in front of the screens.

"As you all know, we've been through so much together," he started. "I just want you all to know how much I truly appreciate everything that everyone has done for the sake of this mission...for coming this far, for sacrificing your livelihoods, and for coming together to fight for your home, your universe, and our God. You can be assured that He is very pleased with having accomplished our mission. All Glory to God!"

"Glory to God!" Everyone cheered.

"In short time, we will be able to pick up transmissions from our universe so that you will be able to reach out to loved ones whom you have left behind, for so long. You will be able to see them and talk to them. Our

God has given us the inspiration to achieve this technology, and it will be operational within hours..."

Again, there were cheers and applause. And within three hours, images of Earth began to flicker onto the overhead screens. This was the first they had seen of their home in years. Before long, incoming and outgoing images and messages were being transmitted, and everyone was eager to have their turn.

Once the first communiqué had been reached on Earth conveying the celestial army's return, a giddy celebration began to spread across the globe and into the heavens. People fell to their knees and praised God and Jesus, not only for the capture of the Kingson Goddess and Lucifer, but for all the restorative efforts following all that had taken place in the Kingson universe. This would only ensure a safe future as well.

After speaking to their loved ones, many of the troops could no longer sleep. Neither could Aaron and Malinch. The shuttles were full of hopeful anticipation. The realization that they were heading home was finally being realized.

CHAPTER 25

THE GLORIOUS RETURN OF THE CELESTIAL ARMADA

Again, the speed and sophistication of the shuttles would become the shining jewel to the celestial fleet. Two times faster than the speed of light they were able to circumvent many of the natural laws that humans were normally bound by.

As the armada approached the edge of the Black Abyss, there were trepid recollections of the perils that confronted them on their first trek through. As they came to the portal opening, they were quickly reminded of how truly immense it was...vast beyond imagination.

Aaron ordered that all the shuttles align themselves in single file, so as to minimize some of the risky encounters they experienced before. But at least they knew what lay ahead.

Once they breached the opening, one of the first hazards they experienced were the drastic changes in temperature, from very hot, to very cold, in unpredictable patterns. Then cosmic winds, carrying debris and dust, made visibility nearly impossible for intermittent periods at a time. At many points, some shuttles narrowly missed huge rocks and asteroids...some of them the size of small moons.

Such conditions might be okay for thrill seekers, but not for an entire fleet only trying to get home. Fortunately, the expert navigational skills of the now seasoned commanders and pilots rendered the ordeal nearly eventless. And although it took a little longer than they expected, they soon made it across the Abyss, and back to their home universe, where everything seemed unusually beautiful and placid.

The final trek, whizzing past the billions of galaxies of our God's awe-inspiring universe, was a sight to behold. The majority of the troops were glued to the windows, taking in the scenery. Some felt as though tourists, sightseeing on vacation.

The final leg of the voyage also rendered a most spectacular view of our Milky Way Galaxy, and the billions of stars that inhabit its vast reaches.

"Now THIS galaxy is familiar to me!!" Malinch announced over the intercom. Everyone cheered, laughed, and cried, at the same time, giving thanks to God for such beauty.

Many reflected at how unimaginable the whole orchestration was, and how only God could've concocted such an unfathomable design.

As the ships entered into the outer arm of our galaxy, they could see our sun, with its nine planets orbiting in a most familiar and tranquilizing recognition. The crew's hearts grew calm, and more tears fell from everyone's eyes.

They passed Pluto, Neptune, Uranus, Saturn, Jupiter and Mars. And although each of those were magnificent in their own right, there wasn't anything quite like the feeling of coming home to the very planet, from where one was created.

Even the sun was as warm and beautiful as ever.

"Everyone follow my lead...!!" Aaron announced to all the other shuttle commanders. He then swooped down, weaving in and out, doing fly-bys across the planetary orbits of Mars and Venus, where human colonies were stationed. The caravan spanned 250 miles long. Lights shone from all the colonies, in jubilant celebration of the armada's return.

Live transmissions were blaring across every onboard speaker. On Earth, live television feeds were pouring in through all network channels. The entire globe was in a festive uproar.

Aaron patched through to his daughter, who was so overwhelmed with joy that she couldn't even speak. Aaron barely recognized her, as she had grown up into a striking young lady. Aaron told her to go to the scheduled landing site, in the Mexican desert, to meet him.

Malinch contacted her family as well, and told them to also meet her at the landing site.

The landing site would be overrun by the families of the celestial troops and personnel.

CHAPTER 26

THE PEOPLE OF EARTH AWAIT THE LANDING OF THEIR LOVED ONES

The landing armada...

It wasn't until nighttime that the armada was scheduled to land, and all the vast desert fields were cleared for the shuttles' landings. Meanwhile family and spectators watched from afar. And people all around the world were eagerly anticipating the arrival of the Celestial Fleet. Even the many nonbelievers of the world stood in silence and awe. Some even started believing. Nevertheless, all were receiving God's blessings on such a momentous event.

As the Celestial ships breached the atmosphere, Aaron ordered one last pass around the earth, as an aerial parade to honor their homecoming. They illuminated the night sky with a spectacle of brilliance. Then, as they coalesced near the desert plains, an assembly of high-ranking officials poised themselves near the airfield, ready to welcome the cast of heroes back to Earth.

Everyone on board was eager to set foot on their home planet, again. Everyone else watching was eager to see them do so. But before Aaron gave the order to disembark, he asked the entire crew to say one more closing prayer, before they landed. Many got down on their knees.

"Father, God, we give you thanks for both giving us our mission and making us victorious. And we also thank you so much for delivering us from this horrific threat, and bringing us back to our native planet, back to our homes, and back to our loved ones...

We thank you for keeping our families safe, and we honor you with great reverence, obedience and love."

They then gave a long moment of silence for all those whom they had lost, for their honor and their bravery.

Then everyone said, "Amen."

Then Aaron gave the last order he would ever give to the Celestial Armies.

"Let's set these ships down, and see our loved ones!!"

A deafening but familiar roar thundered for miles and miles around, at the landing of the shuttles. Malinch was the first to set her craft down. Then came the next, and the next. As each craft landed, the outer hatches opened.

When Aaron and Malinch appeared from on the departure ramp of their ship, the crowd went wild with screaming and applause. They hardly set foot on the ground before they were overtaken and swept up by a mob of jubilant spectators. They were then ushered to a cluster of canopy Ramadas, where a celebratory setting had been waiting, flush with tables of food and champaign. Here, they were met with huge hugs and kisses by their long awaiting families and friends.

Then everyone ate, drank, and became merry.

After hours of celebration and honors, all the troops were required to stay in the base hospital for reassimilation back into the Earthly elements. Then, they would be allowed to go home, with their families.

Everyone that was assigned to that mission was dubbed a Celestial Hero by all the nations of the world. It was an honor that had never been conceived before, and will likely never be again.

That night, the Celestial Shuttles disappeared into the ether as though they were never there in the first place. It was well accepted that they were returned to their Owner, in the Heavens.

✦ 113 ✦

THE WAR ON THE OTHER SIDE OF THE BLACK ABYSS

✦ 114 ✦

EPILOGUE

After a colonial voyage to Mars, Captain Marcus and Caren both retired from their duties and got married somewhere in the mountains near Fresno, California. They are still happily married.

After two weeks of reassimilation, Aaron and Malinch got married, as planned, near one of the Great Lakes, in Michigan, where Malinch grew up. After honeymooning in a colony on Venus, they bought a home in California, where they have lived with Aaron's daughter, Glory, who's now training to be a pilot. A month after they moved in, Malinch found out she was pregnant. It was a baby boy. They named him Zinson.

Not a night would pass that Aaron and Malinch wouldn't get down on their knees and thank God, the

Father for all that He had rewarded them with. They had everything, and they were happy.

In a dream one night, God Spoke to Aaron, saying, "Because of your faith, courage, and actions, there is peace, not just on Earth, but throughout My universe and into the Heavens as well. For this, I thank you, and I will bless and protect you."

There are demons everywhere in this world. Do you have the courage to undertake the mission that God has appointed you?